PAT HUTCHINS

We're Going on a Picnic!

SCHOLASTIC INC.
New York Toronto London Auckland Sydney
Mexico City New Delhi Hong Kong Buenos Aires

ISBN   0-439-48890-7

Copyright © 2002 by Pat Hutchins. All rights reserved. Published by Scholastic Inc., 557 Broadway, New York, NY 10012, by arrangement with Greenwillow Books, an imprint of HarperCollins Publishers. SCHOLASTIC and associated logos are trademarks and/or registered trademarks of Scholastic Inc.

12 11 10 9 8 7 6 5 4 3 2 1   3 4 5 6 7 8/0

Printed in the U.S.A.   08

First Scholastic printing, March 2003

Pen and ink and felt-tipped markers were used to prepare the full color artwork.
The text type is Amway Opti-Regular.

FOR RACHEL ISA BAINES

"Let's go on a picnic,"
said Hen, Duck, and Goose.
"It's such a lovely day!"

So Hen picked some berries
(because Hen liked berries best),
and Goose picked some apples
(because Goose liked apples best),
and Duck picked some pears
(because Duck liked pears best).
And they put them in the basket.

"We're going on a picnic!" they sang
as they walked across the field.

"This looks like a nice place
for a picnic," said Hen,
and set the basket down.
"I can't wait to eat
some of those berries!"

"It's a bit shady," said Duck.
"Let's go up the hill.
 We might find an even nicer place."
"All right," said Hen,
"but it's your turn to carry the basket."

"We're going on a picnic!" they sang
as they walked up the hill.

"This looks like a nice place for a picnic," said Duck, and set the basket down. "I can't wait to eat some of those pears!"

"It's a bit windy," said Goose.
"Let's go down the hill.
 We might find an even nicer place."
"All right," said Duck,
"but it's your turn to carry the basket."

"We're going on a picnic!" they sang
as they walked down the hill.

"This looks like a nice place for a picnic,"
said Goose, and set the basket down.
"I can't wait to eat some of those apples!"

"It's a bit hot," said Hen and Duck.
"Let's go down this path.
 We might find an even nicer place."
"All right," said Goose,
"but let's ALL carry the basket."

"We're going on a picnic!" they sang
as they walked around the lane.

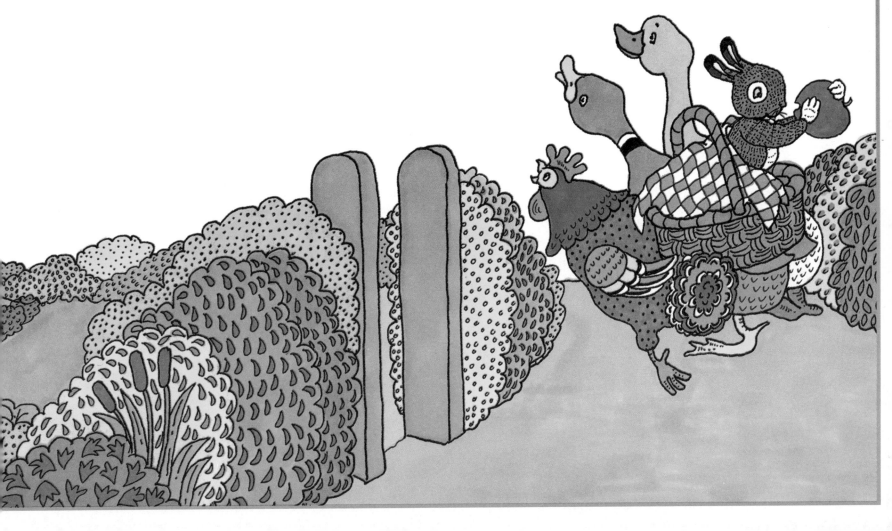

"Oh!" they cried,
and set the basket down.
"We've walked back home,
and we haven't had our picnic!"

"Off we go again," said Hen.
But when they picked up the basket,
it was very light.

And very empty.

"Duck," said Hen, "did you eat the pears?"

"No," said Duck.

"Goose," said Hen, "did you eat the apples?"

"No," said Goose.

"Hen," said Duck and Goose, "did you eat the berries?"

"No," said Hen.

"Then they must have fallen out," said everyone
at the same time.

So Hen picked some more berries
(because Hen liked berries best),
and Goose picked some more apples
(because Goose liked apples best),
and Duck picked some more pears
(because Duck liked pears best).
And they put them in the basket.

"We're going on a picnic!" they sang
as they walked across the field.

"This looks like a nice place for a picnic,"
they all said, and set the basket down.